To:

From:

To my biggest supporters of
whatever I do in life,
a.k.a
The Knebel Team!

FOX HUNT

THE KENTS' QUEST #2

by C. Knebel
Simple Words Books™

Chapter 1

Camp Split Rock

It is the end of fall. Time for the Kents to camp at Split Rock. These trips are so much fun with lots of quests.

At Camp Split Rock, the Kents rent a grass lot for their red tent. The lot is at the back of the camp by a hill. By the lot, there is a big pond with lots of fish.

Tim Kent is ten. He is tall and fit. Kim is Tim's sibling. She is six and likes to do what Tim does. She does not want to be left out of the fun.

Tim and Kim think camping at Split Rock is the best. They like to spend time fishing with their mom and dad.

Tim helps his dad set up the tent on the lot. Step by step, they fix the rods. Next, the walls go up. Then the pegs go in the grass. At last, the tent is up.

Then they hang a string on a branch for a swing. Kim jumps on the swing. She lifts her legs and blasts off fast.

Mrs. Kent brings the cots to the tent. Tim brings the bags from the trunk of the van. Kim jumps off the swing to help Tim.

When the kids unpack the bags, they set up a hand of Go Fish to pass the time. Bud sits next to them.

Bud is the Kents' pup. He is gray with black spots. Bud jumps and runs all the time. He likes these camping trips as well. They are so much fun.

Mr. Kent plans to rent rods at the shop so they can fish in the pond.

"I will check out the fishing shop. I will be back quick," he tells Mrs. Kent.

Bud wags and trots down the path next to him.

At the shop, there is an odd man. He is big and has a red cap with a “C” on it. He looks grim.

The man bumps into Bud.

“I do not like pups!” he grunts and kicks Bud.

Bud yaps and yaps.

Mr. Kent is at the checkout desk.

“What is up with you, Bud? Are you O.K.?” he asks as he pats Bud. “I got the rods. I am all set. Let us go back to the tent.”

The big man gets out of the shop just in front of them. Bud stays next to Mr. Kent. He does not like this man.

Chapter 2

The Missing Bags

Back at the grass lot, as Mrs. Kent preps the grill for the next day's picnic, the shrub next to her shifts.

"Bud, get out of the shrub," she says. But Bud is with Mr. Kent at the fishing shop.

Next, she preps the hot dogs. The bag that had the buns is there. But just half the buns are in it.

"This is odd. Did I pack all the buns?" she thinks. "Or did I just bring half of them with us?"

She checks all the bags. But she cannot spot the rest of the buns.

"Tim, Kim. Did you grab all the bags from the van?" she asks.

"Yes, Mom. I think we got them all," says Kim.

"A bag with half of the buns is lost," Mrs. Kent tells the kids.

Tim sets down his hand of Go Fish.

"Was it in the van with the rest of the bags?" he asks his mom.

"I think so. There must be a bag left in the trunk. Can you check it?" she asks Tim.

Tim runs to the van. But there are no bags left in the trunk.

"Oh, well. I did not pack all the buns then. We got half of them with us. We can just get what we need at the shop," says Mrs. Kent.

Mr. Kent and Bud are back from the shop with the rods. They are all set to fish at the pond the next day.

"It will be a fun day with a picnic," says Mr. Kent.

Bud skips and hops next to Mr. Kent. Mrs. Kent thinks this is odd.

"Was Bud with you all this time?" she asks.

Mr. Kent nods. "He was with me at the shop."

"If it was not Bud in the shrub, what is in there?" Mrs. Kent steps back from the shrub. She gets the chills.

Kim sets down her hand of Go Fish fast. She runs to her dad.

"What can it be, Dad?" she asks.

Mr. Kent checks the shrub. There is not a thing in there. Just a bug on a branch.

"I cannot tell," says Mr. Kent. "A cat?"

"Can it be a big cat?" asks Kim. "Like a bobcat?"

"Do not fret, Kim. There are no bobcats in this camp. We are O.K.," Mr. Kent hugs her.

"Check out the sunset," says Mrs. Kent to shift the topic. "Let me get this stuff set for the next day. What do you want for brunch at the picnic?" she asks.

“Hot dogs for brunch! Can I have a hot dog with a bun?” asks Tim.

Mrs. Kent nods.

“I want hot dogs as well. With chips and no buns!” Kim jumps in. “Can I bring a bag of chips to the tent to snack on, Mom?” she adds.

“No, hon. It is time for bed,” she tells Kim.

“But I do not want to go to bed yet!” Kim grunts.

“Kim, it will be so much fun to rest in the tent. You get to pick your cot if you are in the tent fast," Tim distracts Kim.

Kim forgets the chips and the bobcats. Mrs. Kent winks at Tim.

Tim acts as if he will grab Kim. Kim gets a kick out of this.

"Last kid to the tent is a skunk," Kim yells as she runs to the tent.

Tim sprints like a flash.

Mrs. Kent packs the hot dogs and chips in the picnic basket.

Mr. Kent sets the rods next to a big

bucket. He plans to fill the bucket with lots of fish from the pond.

When Mr. and Mrs. Kent are all set with their tasks, they get into the tent to be with the kids.

The day ends with no big mess.

Chapter 3

A Fox Cub

The next day, Kim is up with the sun. She cannot stay still in her cot. She gets up and out of the tent.

It is crisp out. Kim has her flip flops on. The wet grass chills her. She grabs her jacket.

Just then, she spots a small fox in the shrub next to the tent. The fox cub is in their picnic pack!

"Psst! Get out of the basket!" she yells. "Mom! Dad! Help! A fox is in the snacks!"

Tim jumps out of his cot. Mr. and Mrs. Kent run out of the tent in their PJs.

Kim's yell shocks the cub. He stands still for a bit. Then he blasts off like a rocket.

"Oh, no! Check this out," says Mr. Kent.

The picnic basket is a big mess.

"There are no buns left for the hot dogs. Just a bunch of bits," he adds.

"It must be this fox that got half of the buns as well," Kim says.

"Oh, well," says Tim. "I am glad it is just a small cub. What if it was a big bobcat?" asks Tim.

He is not upset with the fox.

"A big bobcat is bad. A small fox, not that much. Not just for snacks, but for us as well," he adds.

"We still can have a fun picnic. Plus, we can get buns in the shop if we need to," says Mrs. Kent.

"What if the fox is back when we are by the pond?" Kim asks.

"Do not fuss, Kim. Mom and Dad say we are O.K.," Tim cuts in. "And we can lock all the stuff in the tent so not a thing will be out if the fox is back."

"Yep! It is what it is. Let us fix the snacks for the picnic," Mrs. Kent tells Kim.

"Kim and I can fix the hot dogs," says Tim.

"Well, then. We have all we need for flap-jacks. If you help your mom with the hot dogs, I will get on with the flap-jacks," says Mr. Kent.

Tim is glad for that. He thinks flap-jacks are the best.

Mr. Kent sets up the grill for the hot dogs and the flap-jacks.

"Let us go to the pond," says Tim to Kim. "You pick up the drinks. I will get the chips and a blanket."

Mr. Kent grabs the rods and the bucket. Mrs. Kent packs the hot dogs and the flap-jacks.

She locks up what is left of the snacks. She zips the tent. She does not want the fox to get his hands on their stuff if he is back.

But she forgets to lock up Bud’s snacks.

Chapter 4

The Fox Is Back

The Kents go down to the pond. Bud sprints next to them.

The picnic is a hit. They have lots of fun in the sun.

Back at the camp, the fox is by the tent. This time, he dips into Bud's snacks.

The Kents are back from the pond with lots of fish to grill. When they get to the tent, the lot is a mess! Bud yips. His snack bag is in rags.

"The fox was back. He snuck into Bud's snacks," Kim yells.

"How much did he get this time?" asks Mrs. Kent.

"We do not have much left for Bud," Kim says. She is upset with the fox.

"Bud's snacks are a quick fix. We will just pick a bag from the shelf in the shop," says Mr. Kent.

Kim pets Bud on his chin. She can tell Bud is sad.

Tim spots the fox next to a big shrub. The cub runs into a den. He is fast.

"Tim, where did the fox go?" asks Mrs. Kent.

Tim lifts his hand to the left where the hill is. "He went in that den next to the big shrub on the hill."

"What is a den?" Kim asks.

"A den is a pit where the fox stays," says Tim.

"Mom, I want to check on him. He may need help. Can I go to the fox's den?" asks Tim.

Mrs. Kent looks at the hill where the den is.

"No. I do not want you to go to the den by yourself," Mrs. Kent tells Tim.

Kim does not get why Tim is not mad at the fox.

"Tim, the fox got the snacks. And you think he needs help?" snaps Kim. "We need help. Not him. Why are you not upset with him?"

"He is just a cub, Kim. A cub needs to have a mom or dad with him. But he was all by himself. Mom, I think he needs help," insists Tim.

Kim nods. She did not think of it this way.

"I can go with Tim. Can we check on the cub, Mom?" asks Kim.

She wants to help the cub as well.

"O.K., kids. You can go to the den. Tim, you must stay with Kim. And Kim, stay next to Tim. Got it?" asks Mrs. Kent. "Be back at the tent fast. And do not forget the bell, Kim. Ring it if you need help."

Kim hangs the bell on her belt.

Tim packs six fish in a bag for the fox. He grabs Kim's hand. They run up the hill to the den.

Chapter 5

Pip The Fox

Tim gets down flat on the sand and scans the den. He spots the fox at the back. The cub stands still. He is in stress and is upset.

"It is O.K.," Tim says.

He picks a fish from the bag and casts it out to the fox. The fox sniffs the fish and then gulps it down.

"We want to help you," Tim adds. He sets his hand out for the fox to sniff. "Kim did not want you to panic."

Then, he hands the next fish to the cub. The cub gulps down this fish as well.

"Fish, at last," says the fox.

Tim jumps up. He does not expect the fox to say a thing back to him.

"So glad you can chat with us," Kim jumps in. "I am Kim. And this is Tim."

She can tell the fox is sad. She is sad that she upset him with her yells back by the tent.

"I am Pip," says the cub.

"Hi, Pip," Kim says.

"It was bad that I ran off with the buns and the snacks," blasts the cub. "But I am not a bad fox."

"Why did you run off with them?" asks Kim.

"I… I need lunch. I cannot hunt yet," the fox says with his chin down.

"Did you like the snacks?" asks Kim. She wants to get a grin out of the cub.

"Well, I like fish, frogs and eggs. But I get what I can," says Pip.

"We got lots of fish for you in this bag," Tim says.

He sets the bag on the sand. Pip jumps on the bag. He is glad that there are lots of fresh fish for him.

"This is the best snack I have had in days!" says Pip.

"Where is your mom? Where is your dad?" Kim asks. "Why are you not with them?"

The fox is sad.

"A big man set a trap next to the den. Mom and Dad got stuck in the net. The next day, the man got them out. I did not see where they went," the cub sobs. "What if the man kills Mom and Dad?"

"No. No. I do not think he will kill them," Kim insists.

Tim pets Pip's back. "We can help you."

"Can you?" asks Pip.

"Yes, I think so. With help from Mom and Dad," says Kim.

Pip, Tim and Kim run back to the camp. Mr. and Mrs. Kent are by the tent.

Mr. Kent brings a drink and fresh fish in a dish to the cub. Pip gulps them down and tells the Kents of his mom and dad, the trap they were stuck in and the big man that got them.

“There must be hints by the trap,” says Mr. Kent. “Let us check out where the net was.”

“Do you think we can help Pip?” Kim asks her mom.

“Where there is a will, there is a way!” says Mrs. Kent. “Pack up kids. We will track down this bad man!”

Chapter 6

Cabin On The Hill

The Kents, Bud and the cub go to the spot where Pip's mom and dad got stuck. There is no trap, no net and no fox.

"What can you tell us? What did the man look like?" asks Tim.

"He was big. He had a cap when he got my mom and dad out of the net. It was a red cap with a "C" on it. The next day, he was back with a black run down truck with a pen in the back."

"Where did the truck go?" asks Mr. Kent.

Pip shrugs.

"It had a bad smell to it. Does that help?" asks Pip.

"All hints help," grins Mr. Kent. He pets the cub.

Mrs. Kent spots red dots on a shrub's trunk. She thinks this is odd.

Bud runs down the hill. He sniffs the shrubs, the grass and the mud. Then he yaps with a thrill.

What did Bud spot?

Can it be a hint in the mud?

Tim runs to Bud fast. There are lots of prints in the mud.

"Mom! Dad! Pip!" Tim yells. "Check this out!"

"Are they your mom's or dad's prints?" asks Kim. "Do they smell like them? What do you think?"

Pip sniffs the prints in the mud.

"Yes! This is Mom's print!" Then he sniffs the next print. "And this is Dad's!"

Plus, there are prints from a big man. But no tracks of a truck.

"If your mom's and dad's prints are in this path, the man must not have got them on the truck. They must be just steps from us," says Tim.

"Pip's mom and dad must be this way!" yells Kim. "The prints go west."

Pip and Bud stay on the path with the tracks.

They end up at a cabin at the top of the hill. A swing is on the deck.

There is a bad smell. A trash bin with a big crack sticks out of a pit in the mud. The bog by the cabin has a distinct smell.

"Can you still smell your mom's and dad's prints?" asks Mr. Kent.

Pip says no in a sad way. "The bog stinks so much. I cannot smell a thing to track them."

A big black truck with a pen in the back stands in front of the cabin. It has a dent in the front from a crash. There is a big "C" on the back of the truck.

"Does the cabin or the truck ring a bell?" asks Mrs. Kent.

"This is it! That is the truck by the net," yells Pip. "And… and the truck had this bad smell."

Kim grabs her mom's hand. She does not like the feel of this cabin.

Tim sticks to his mom and grabs her hand as well.

They wish to get out of there fast.

Chapter 7

Man With The Gun

"Let us check if the man is in the cabin." Mr. Kent taps on the door. Kim and Tim stand still.

A big man with a red cap is at the door.

"Yes?" snaps the man. "What do you want?" He has a handgun in his belt.

Bud yaps. This is the bad man in the fishing shop.

Tim gets a cramp in his gut.

“I bet he has Pip’s mom and dad,” he thinks.

“Oh, well, Mr…?” Mr. Kent kicks off the chat.

“Crock. I am Chuck Crock. And you are?” he asks.

“Oh, I am Tom Kent. And Kim, Tim and Mrs. Kent.” Mr. Kent stands tall as he asks, “Mr. Crock, are you the man that set the fox traps by Camp Split Rock?”

The big man has a grim look. He does not say a thing.

“This is Pip. His mom and dad got stuck in a trap next to their den,” says Tim.

“Pip is just a cub!” adds Kim. “He still needs his mom and dad.”

“Do you have them? Are they in this cabin?” asks Mrs. Kent.

“Why do you ask?” he yells.

“We want them back,” says Tim.

“Is that so?” grunts Chuck Crock.

He steps out of his cabin.

Tim gets the chills. He feels like a speck next to this big man.

Chuck Crock stops in front of Mrs. Kent. She does not like that.

As she backs off, she trips on a rock and falls on her back in the mud.

The man grabs her hand to help her up. She checks out his hand. He has red spots on his hand.

She thinks of the red dots on the trunk of the shrub by the den.

"Did you cut your hand?" she asks.

"It is just red ink," the man says. "I tag the shrubs with my traps with red ink. So I can spot them fast."

"So it was you," Mr. Kent says. "We need Pip's mom and dad back."

"Well, you got me. Let me ask you this. What is in it for me?" the man grins.

Mr. Kent shrugs. "It is just the best thing to do. That is it."

"I will not hand them back to you. I want to sell them," blasts the big man.

Pip gasps. It is as if the man drops a bomb. Pip feels sick when he thinks this bad man will sell them.

What if he cannot get them back!

Mrs. Kent jumps in. "Sell? Who can you sell them to?"

"A rich king," says the man. "I hit the jackpot with this king. He pays lots of cash for them. He wants to have them as pets."

"Will you tell the king how you trap them?" Mr. Kent asks.

"No! No! No!" The man gets upset.

"If I tell the king, he will not get them from me. And I want that cash. I tell you, man! You do not want to mess with me. Just get off my land! Get out when you can!"

Chapter 8

The Hut

Bang!

The door slams fast.

"Until next time, Mr. Crock," yells Mr. Kent as he steps back from the cabin.

They all go to the back of the cabin.

"He got your mom and dad," says Mrs. Kent.

Pip's chin drops to his chest.

"I will not see them, will I?" he sobs. "There is not much we can do."

"This cannot be the end. There must be a way. What do we do next?" Kim asks.

"If they are in the cabin, how can we get in when the man is still there?" asks Tim.

"I do not think they are in the cabin," says Mr. Kent.

"But then, where is Mom and Dad?" asks Pip.

Tim and Kim shrug. But Mr. Kent has a hunch.

"This is not as bad as you think," says Mr. Kent. "In fact, I have a plan, kids."

"What is your plan, Dad?" Kim asks. "Tell us. Tell us."

"Did you spot the hut next to the cabin?" says Mr. Kent.

Tim and Kim nod.

"There are pens in front of the hut. I bet Pip's mom and dad are in there. Let us check it out," says Mr. Kent.

"What if they are not in the hut?" asks Pip.

He gets the chills when he thinks his mom and dad may be on a ship on their way to the king.

Mr. Kent thinks Pip is just a cub and this must be a lot for him.

He pets Pip's back. "They are in the hut. Just trust us."

"We will not let you down." Mrs. Kent sits next to Pip. "If he will sell them, he will tend to them well. So he can get lots of cash for them."

Chapter 9

The Lock

The Kents, Bud and Pip slink to the hut.

"Oh, no!" yelps Pip.

There is a big lock. They cannot get in.

"If we get rid of the lock, we will get them out of there," says Tim.

"We can smash the lock with a rock," Kim says. She picks up a rock.

“Just be still for a sec, Kim. Let us think,” says Mr. Kent. “If we slam the lock, Chuck Crock will pick up on what we are up to. And we do not want that. Do we?”

“No, we do not,” say Kim and Tim.

“Just think. What can we do?” Mr. Kent is stuck.

He does not have an end to the plan.

Kim shrugs.

“If we cannot crack the lock, we can get Chuck Crock to unlock it for us.” Tim lifts his fist.

"Him? Unlock it for us? Are you nuts?" asks Kim. "How do we get him to do that?"

Tim picks a pack of gum out of his pocket. "Dad, this was in that film on TV. The cop stuck his gum in the lock. The door did not lock up when it shut. What do you think? Can we do that?"

"Oh, yes. It was Top Cop! It was on TV last spring," says Mrs. Kent with a grin.

"That is it. We got a plan!" says Mr. Kent.

"This is what we do. When Mr. Crock brings drinks and lunch to the hut,

Tim, you run to the hut. Then you fix the gum on the lock. Do not rush with the gum. You got to be spot on. When it is set, run back as fast as you can," Mr. Kent says.

They sit at the back of the hut.

In just a bit, the man exits his cabin. He grabs a bin.

He fills it to the rim with fish and frogs from a chest next to the pond. He hand cranks up a bucket out of the well.

"That bucket must be for your mom and dad," Mrs. Kent tells Pip.

Chuck Crock unlocks the hut and brings in the bucket and the bin.

Mr. Kent nods at Tim. “Go for it, Son. You can do this. Quick! Run. Run. Run.”

Tim gets that this is a big task. He sprints to the hut. He sticks the gum in the lock and checks that it is set. Then, he runs back as fast as he can in the nick of time.

Mr. Kent pats Tim on the back. “Let us just be still until he is back in his cabin.”

When the man is out of the hut, the door shuts. The lock clicks, but it does not lock all the way.

Chuck Crock flings the bucket next to the chest. It hits the bin with a big bang.

Kim jumps when the bucket hits the chest. And the bell on her belt clings. The man checks out the cling. But he does not spot a thing. So he gets back into his cabin.

Chapter 10

The Big Scam

"Let us get your mom and dad out of there," says Mrs. Kent.

When they get in, what is in the hut shocks them.

The bad man has a big set up in this hut.

Pip's mom and dad are in a pen by the wall. A big whip hangs on the wall.

But that is not all.

There are lots of pets stuck in pens as well. Cats, pups and ducks. How can this be?

When Pip spots his mom and dad, he sprints to their pen. He wags and jumps up and down in front of them. Tim runs with Pip. He unlocks the pen and gets them out.

"Let us get all the pets out of this hut!" says Mrs. Kent. "Kim! Tim! Tom! Quick! I need a hand."

They all rush to help.

Tim unlocks the pens on the top shelf. Six pups run to Bud and sit next to him.

Tim's dad unlocks the ducks. They quack as they run out of the pens.

Kim gets to the rest of the pens. The pets rush out of the hut fast.

"We got them all. Let us go," says Mr. Kent.

They all run out of the hut and sprint back to Camp Split Rock. The fox clan sticks with the Kents. Six pups tag on as well. The rest of the pets go their ways.

Just as they run down the hill, they run into a trap with a skunk stuck in a net. Mr. Kent rips the net and the skunk jumps out. But he cannot run. The net has cut his leg.

"This is a big scam," says Mr. Kent as he picks up the skunk.

"This cannot go on," adds Mrs. Kent. "We must tell the cops what this man is up to! We will need their help."

"Let us call them when we are back at camp," says Mr. Kent.

"No, Dad!" say Tim and Kim. "Call the cops now! That bad man can run off when he grasps that the pets have left."

"Yes, it is best if I call the cops now," says Mr. Kent.

"Hi. 9-1-1? This is Tom Kent. There is a pet scam by Camp Split Rock. A man traps pets to sell them for cash to a king. He is Mr. Crock," says Mr. Kent. "Yes! Yes! Chuck Crock. We got all the pets out of his hut. Ten pets are still with us. You can pick them up at Camp Split Rock. We are on the grass lot at the back of the camp. We got a big red tent. You cannot miss it."

Mr. Kent tells the cops where Mr. Crock's cabin is. "Hmm. Glad to be of help," he adds and hangs up.

"Tell us, Dad. What did the cops say?" ask Kim and Tim.

"They are glad to pin him down. Chuck Crock was on their list. The cops are on their way to the cabin," tells Mr. Kent. "Let us get back to the camp fast. A cop will stop by to pick up the pets."

Chapter 11

Back at Camp

Back at camp, Mrs. Kent tends to the skunk's cut.

Kim grabs cups with drinks for all. She brings a big pan for the pets to drink from as well.

Tim and Kim sit on a bench to rest. They gulp down the drinks.

Bud jumps on Kim's lap and has a nap. The pups jump next to Bud as well.

Pip is glad, at last. He is with his mom and dad and the cops will get the bad man.

"What a day!" says Mrs. Kent.

"I got my mom and dad back thanks to you all," says Pip.

He jumps on Tim's lap. Tim hugs Pip.

"Thank you for your help," says Pip's mom.

"I am glad that we met Pip," says Mrs. Kent.

"Well, there is not much we can do until the cops get to the camp," says Mr. Kent as he tends the pets.

"Can Kim and I chill out by the pond?" asks Tim. "We can fish as well. We need lots of fish. We got a big gang to grill for."

"It is best if we all stay by the tent until the cops get to the camp," says Mr. Kent.

Tim nods. He does not go to the pond. He wants to be by the tent when the cops get there.

Chapter 12

Fox Hunt Ends

Just then, a big black van stops by the tent. A cop gets out.

"Hi, there. Are you Tom Kent?" asks the cop.

Mr. Kent nods. "Glad you can stop by so quick to pick them up."

The cop checks out the pets.

"The skunk's leg is well. They all look fit," he says with a grin. "Thanks for all the help. I want to tell you that we got Chuck Crock. He will not trap pets for a long time."

"He is a con man," rants Mr. Kent with disgust.

"I am with you, Mr. Kent," says the cop. "We met him in the spring. He was odd. We got a hunch that he was up to no good. But we did not think he had a hand in this big scam. So we did not track him down. We did not think it was this bad. But the hut says it all. Thanks to you, we got him!"

Kim claps with bliss.

"Next big task is to track all the traps and get rid of them. And we will need lots of help. We do not want this to go on," adds the cop.

Mrs. Kent jumps in the chat. "Tom, did you tell the cops how he tags the shrubs?"

"Oh, no. I forgot that," says Mr. Kent.

"You must check the shrubs for the red dots," insists Mrs. Kent. "He tags the trunk of the shrubs with red ink dots when he hangs up his traps."

The cop jots down what she says. "This is a big help, Mrs. Kent. Thank you for the hint. Let me ask you this. How did you get the pets out of the hut?

Chuck Crock says there was a lock. Was there not?"

"Yes," says Tim. "There was. When Chuck Crock went in the hut, I stuck gum in the lock."

"Oh, just like in the film Top Cop!" says the cop.

"Yes! Yes!" says Tim with a thrill.

"What a plan!" says the cop with a grin. "This is a heck of a gang you got, Mr. and Mrs. Kent."

Tim winks at his mom and dad.

"We will lock him up for a long time thanks to you," adds the cop.

"I do not wish him ill. But we all get what we ask for," says Mrs. Kent.

"Glad you got him," nods Mr. Kent.

"That is my job," says the cop. "And we are off to get the next bad man."

Pip, his mom and his dad run up the hill to their den.

The cop picks up the pups and the skunk. He sets them in the pens in the trunk of his van. But this time the pets are in good hands.

All are glad that the cops end this scam at last.

You can download full color

CERTIFICATE OF ACCOMPLISHMENT

and

CERTIFICATE OF COMPLETION

on our website

SIMPLEWORDSBOOKS.COM

Certificate of Accomplishment

This certificate is awarded to

____

for successful completion of

Fox Hunt

SIMPLE WORDS

______________ Signature

__________ Date

FOX HUNT

WORD LIST

You can download the full word list on our website

simplewordsbooks.com

#	Word	Count
1	a	153
2	acts	1
3	adds	9
4	all	31
5	am	9
6	an	2
7	and	110
8	are	47
9	as	31
10	ask	5
11	asks	41
12	at	33
13	back	42
14	backs	1
15	bad	15
16	bag	11
17	bags	6
18	bang	2
19	basket	3
20	be	26
21	bed	2
22	bell	4
23	belt	3
24	bench	1
25	best	6

#	Word	Count
26	bet	2
27	big	35
28	bin	4
29	bit	2
30	bits	1
31	black	4
32	blanket	1
33	blasts	4
34	bliss	1
35	bobcat	3
36	bobcats	2
37	bog	2
38	bomb	1
39	branch	2
40	bring	2
41	brings	6
42	brunch	2
43	bucket	8
44	Bud	35
45	bug	1
46	bumps	1
47	bun	1
48	bunch	1
49	buns	11
50	but	21

#	Word	Count
51	by	22
52	cabin	18
53	call	3
54	camp	16
55	camping	2
56	can	45
57	cannot	12
58	cap	4
59	cash	4
60	casts	1
61	cat	2
62	cats	1
63	chat	3
64	check	11
65	checkout	1
66	checks	6
67	chest	4
68	chill	1
69	chills	4
70	chin	3
71	chips	5
72	Chuck	12
73	clan	1
74	claps	1
75	clicks	1

#	Word	Count
76	cling	1
77	clings	1
78	con	1
79	cop	15
80	cops	12
81	cot	3
82	cots	1
83	crack	2
84	cramp	1
85	cranks	1
86	crash	1
87	crisp	1
88	Crock	18
89	cub	20
90	cups	1
91	cut	3
92	cuts	1
93	dad	41
94	day	9
95	days	1
96	deck	1
97	den	14
98	dent	1
99	desk	1
100	did	23

#	Word	Count
101	dips	1
102	disgust	1
103	dish	1
104	distinct	1
105	distracts	1
106	do	36
107	does	15
108	dog	1
109	dogs	9
110	door	5
111	dots	4
112	down	19
113	drink	2
114	drinks	4
115	drops	2
116	ducks	2
117	eggs	1
118	end	5
119	ends	1
120	exits	1
121	expect	1
122	fact	1
123	fall	1
124	falls	1
125	fast	13

#	Word	Count
126	feel	1
127	feels	2
128	fill	1
129	fills	1
130	film	2
131	fish	21
132	fishing	4
133	fist	1
134	fit	2
135	fix	5
136	flap-jacks	5
137	flash	1
138	flat	1
139	flings	1
140	flip	1
141	flops	1
142	for	41
143	forget	1
144	forgets	2
145	forgot	1
146	fox	32
147	fresh	2
148	fret	1
149	frogs	2
150	from	16

#	Word	Count
151	front	6
152	fun	7
153	fuss	1
154	gang	2
155	gasps	1
156	get	39
157	gets	14
158	glad	11
159	go	24
160	good	2
161	got	28
162	grab	2
163	grabs	8
164	grasps	1
165	grass	6
166	gray	1
167	grill	4
168	grim	2
169	grin	4
170	grins	2
171	grunts	3
172	gulp	1
173	gulps	3
174	gum	6
175	gut	1
176	had	6
177	half	5
178	hand	16
179	handgun	1
180	hands	3
181	hang	1
182	hangs	4
183	has	12
184	have	13
185	he	108
186	heck	1
187	help	23
188	helps	1
189	her	18
190	hi	3
191	hill	9
192	him	19
193	himself	1
194	hint	2
195	hints	2
196	his	36
197	hit	2
198	hits	2
199	hmm	1
200	hon	1
201	hops	1
202	hot	10
203	how	7
204	hugs	2
205	hunch	2
206	hunt	1
207	hut	20
208	I	65
209	if	24
210	ill	1
211	in	87
212	ink	3
213	insists	3
214	into	7
215	is	119
216	it	55
217	jacket	1
218	jackpot	1
219	job	1
220	jots	1
221	jump	1
222	jumps	15
223	just	25
224	Kent	104
225	Kents	9

#	Word	Count
226	kick	1
227	kicks	2
228	kid	1
229	kids	6
230	kill	1
231	kills	1
232	Kim	77
233	king	6
234	land	1
235	lap	2
236	last	6
237	left	8
238	leg	2
239	legs	1
240	let	17
241	lifts	3
242	like	14
243	likes	2
244	list	1
245	lock	16
246	locks	1
247	long	2
248	look	3
249	looks	2
250	lost	1

#	Word	Count
251	lot	8
252	lots	13
253	lunch	2
254	mad	1
255	man	39
256	may	2
257	me	8
258	mess	4
259	met	2
260	miss	1
261	mom	44
262	Mr.	66
263	Mrs.	44
264	much	9
265	mud	6
266	must	12
267	my	5
268	nap	1
269	need	12
270	needs	4
271	net	8
272	next	34
273	nick	1
274	no	23
275	nod	1

#	Word	Count
276	nods	7
277	not	58
278	now	2
279	nuts	1
280	O.K.	5
281	odd	5
282	of	78
283	off	10
284	oh	9
285	on	48
286	or	4
287	out	43
288	pack	5
289	packs	3
290	pan	1
291	panic	1
292	pass	1
293	path	3
294	pats	2
295	pays	1
296	pegs	1
297	pen	5
298	pens	6
299	pet	1
300	pets	20

#	Word	Count
301	pick	7
302	picks	5
303	picnic	9
304	pin	1
305	Pip	44
306	pit	2
307	PJs	1
308	plan	5
309	plans	2
310	plus	2
311	pocket	1
312	pond	11
313	preps	2
314	print	2
315	prints	7
316	psst	1
317	pup	1
318	pups	6
319	quack	1
320	quests	1
321	quick	5
322	rags	1
323	ran	1
324	rants	1
325	red	12

#	Word	Count
326	rent	2
327	rest	6
328	rich	1
329	rid	2
330	rim	1
331	ring	2
332	rips	1
333	rock	10
334	rocket	1
335	rods	6
336	run	18
337	runs	9
338	rush	3
339	sad	5
340	sand	2
341	say	6
342	says	70
343	scam	4
344	scans	1
345	sec	1
346	see	2
347	sell	6
348	set	11
349	sets	7
350	she	46

#	Word	Count
351	shelf	2
352	shift	1
353	shifts	1
354	ship	1
355	shocks	2
356	shop	11
357	shrub	10
358	shrubs	5
359	shrug	1
360	shrugs	3
361	shut	1
362	shuts	1
363	sibling	1
364	sick	1
365	sit	3
366	sits	2
367	six	4
368	skips	1
369	skunk	7
370	slam	1
371	slams	1
372	slink	1
373	small	3
374	smash	1
375	smell	7

#	Word	Count
376	snack	3
377	snacks	11
378	snaps	2
379	sniff	1
380	sniffs	4
381	snuck	1
382	so	16
383	sobs	2
384	son	1
385	speck	1
386	spend	1
387	split	7
388	spot	7
389	spots	7
390	spring	2
391	sprint	1
392	sprints	4
393	stand	1
394	stands	4
395	stay	5
396	stays	2
397	step	2
398	steps	4
399	sticks	4
400	still	11

#	Word	Count
401	stinks	1
402	stop	2
403	stops	2
404	stress	1
405	string	1
406	stuck	9
407	stuff	3
408	sun	2
409	sunset	1
410	swing	4
411	tag	2
412	tags	2
413	tall	2
414	taps	1
415	task	2
416	tasks	1
417	tell	13
418	tells	9
419	ten	2
420	tend	1
421	tends	2
422	tent	25
423	thank	2
424	thanks	4
425	that	33

#	Word	Count
426	the	434
427	their	14
428	them	42
429	then	14
430	there	36
431	these	2
432	they	36
433	thing	7
434	think	17
435	thinks	9
436	this	55
437	thrill	2
438	Tim	80
439	time	13
440	to	128
441	Tom	5
442	top	4
443	topic	1
444	track	4
445	tracks	2
446	trap	8
447	traps	5
448	trash	1
449	trips	3
450	trots	1

#	Word	Count
451	truck	9
452	trunk	7
453	trust	1
454	TV	2
455	unlock	2
456	unlocks	4
457	unpack	1
458	until	4
459	up	34
460	upset	6
461	us	26
462	van	6
463	wags	2
464	wall	2
465	walls	1
466	want	17
467	wants	4
468	was	23
469	way	8
470	ways	1
471	we	69
472	well	22
473	went	3
474	were	1
475	west	1

#	Word	Count
476	wet	1
477	what	34
478	when	21
479	where	13
480	whip	1
481	who	1
482	why	5
483	will	29
484	winks	2
485	wish	2
486	with	68
487	yaps	4
488	yell	1
489	yells	9
490	yelps	1
491	yep	1
492	yes	11
493	yet	2
494	yips	1
495	you	72
496	your	13
497	yourself	1
498	zips	1
Total Words		**5392**

Do you want to write your own story now?

Written by:

Do you want to draw your own story now?

Illustrated by:

EARLY LEVEL CHAPTER BOOKS

www.simplewordsbooks.com

HIGHER LEVEL CHAPTER BOOKS

STUDY GUIDES

DIGITAL COPIES OF OUR BOOKS:

simplewordsbooks.teachable.com

VISIT OUR WEBSITE FOR FREE RESOURCES

simplewordsbooks.com

AND CHECK OUT OUR FREE ONLINE SUMMITS

Manufactured by Amazon.ca
Bolton, ON

23903703R00060